P9-CCI-064

# clowning around

Cathryn Falwell

Orchard Books New York

Orchard Books
A division of Franklin Watts, Inc.
387 Park Avenue South, New York, NY 10016

Manufactured in Hong Kong. Printed and bound by Toppan Printing Co., Inc.
Book design by Cathryn Falwell
The illustrations are cut paper collage.

10 9 8 7 6 5 4 3 2 1

Library of Congress Cataloging-in-Publication Data

Falwell, Cathryn. Clowning around / Cathryn Falwell. p. cm.
Summary: A clown plays with letters and shapes
to create a variety of words and pictures.
ISBN 0-531-05952-9. — ISBN 0-531-08552-X (lib. bdg.)
[1. Vocabulary—Fiction. 2. Shape—Fiction. 3. Clowns—Fiction.] I. Title.
PZ7.F198Cl 1991 [E]—dc20 90-29064

Thanks, Sandy
FOR
David and Anita

clowning

l n o g

i

w

go

go!

go

dgo

dog
dog

dog
dog

doll
doll

doll boll

ball

ball

ball

bal

bar

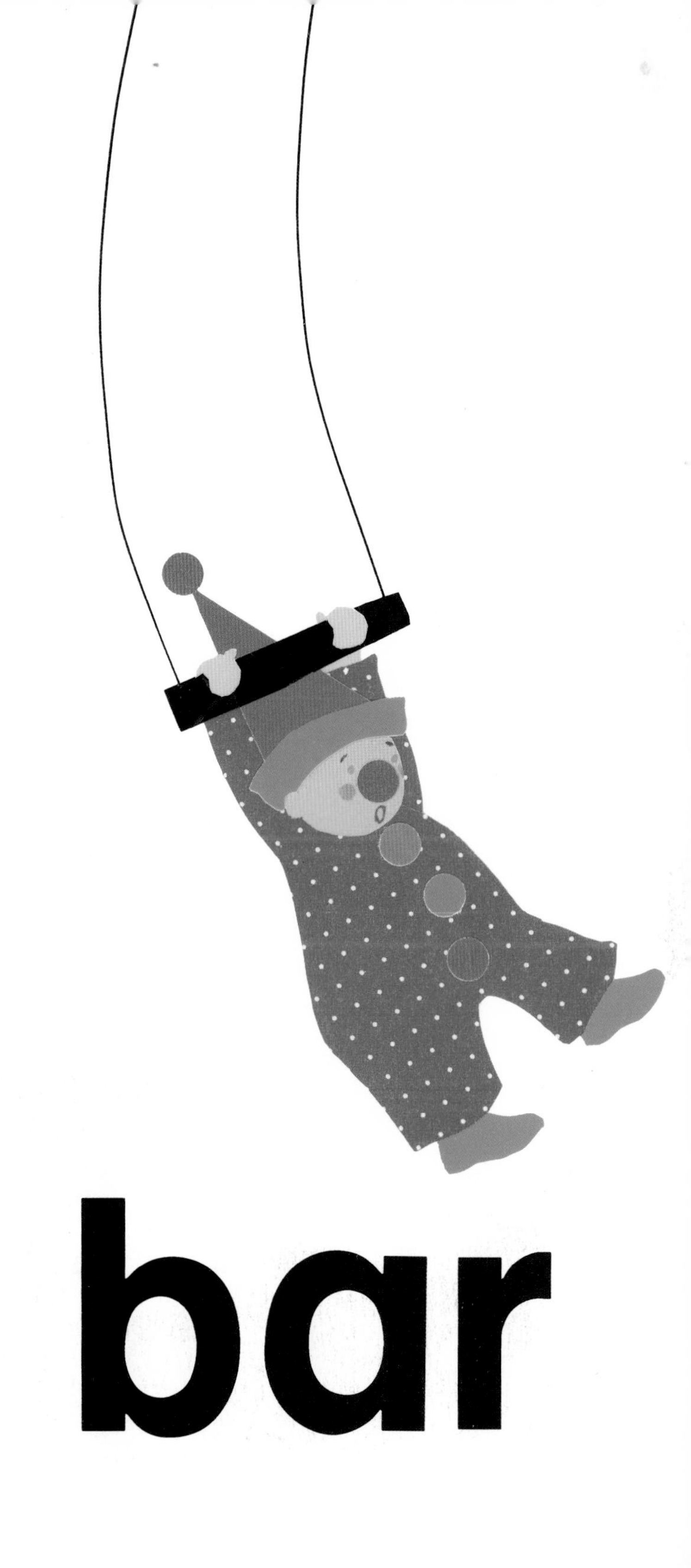

bar

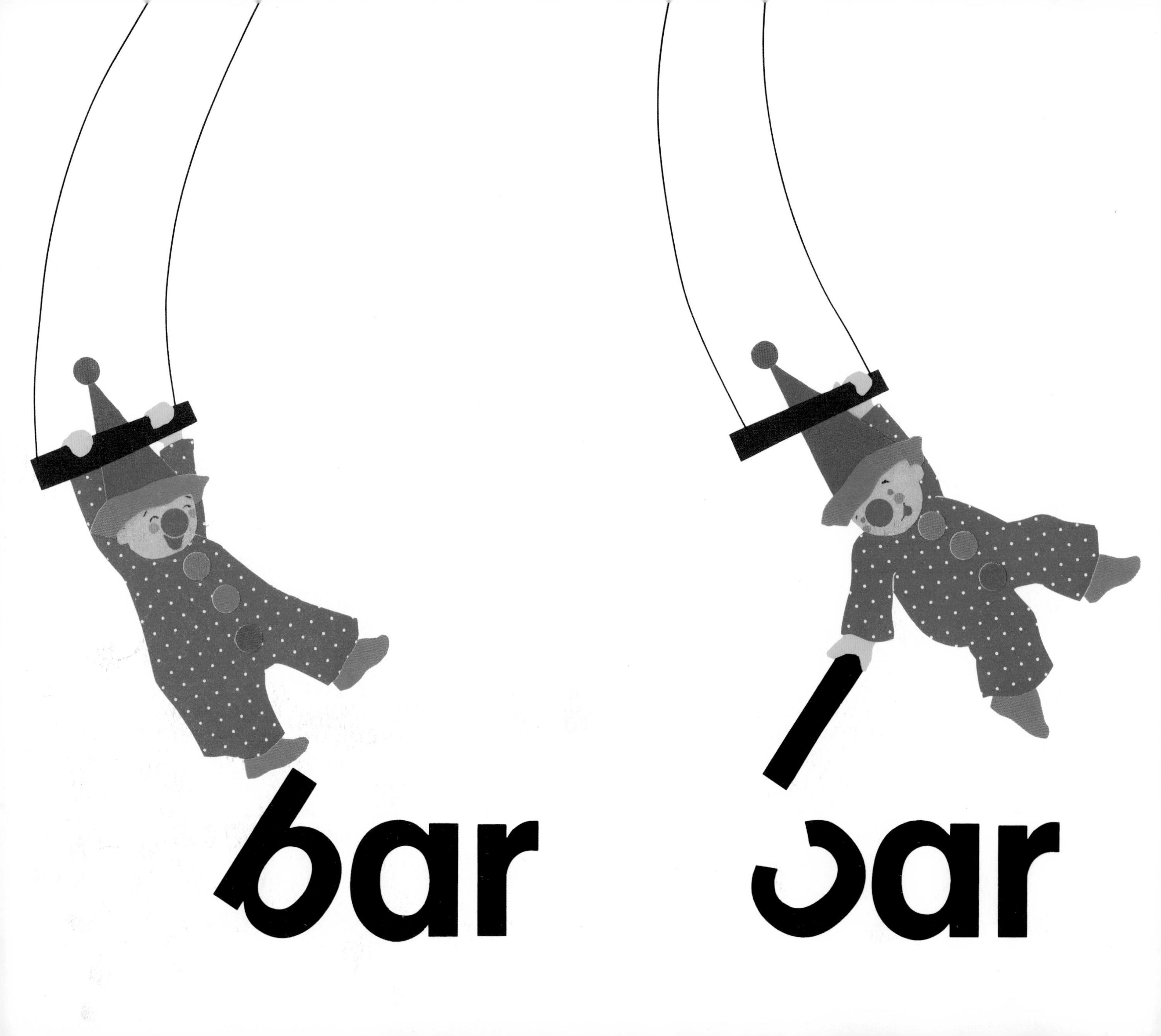
bar

car
car

car
c r

# c r

cro

crowd

# crowd clowd

clown clown

clown clown

clown

bow

bow

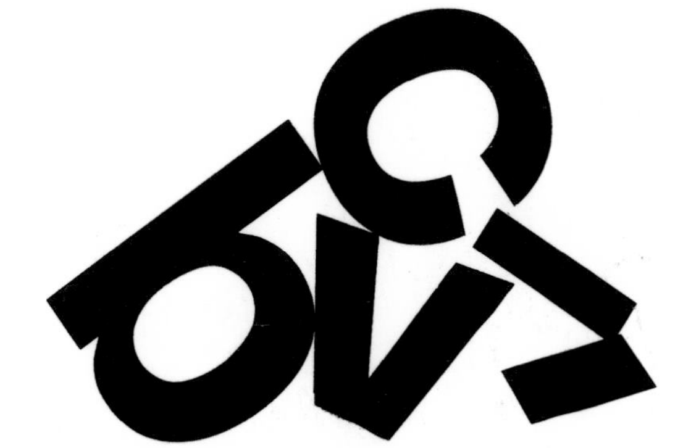

bye